Chimps – very easy books for beginners
Large type
Short words
Short sentences
An illustration on every page
And fun!

This is the second **Chimp**
Look out for more

Frank Mulligan

COOKIE and CURLEY

Illustrated by Terry Myler

THE CHILDREN'S PRESS

To my Mum and Dad

First published 2002 by
The Children's Press
45 Palmerston Road, Dublin 6

2 4 6 8 7 5 3 1

© Text Frank Mulligan 2002
© Illustrations Terry Myler 2002

ISBN 1 901737 38 1

Typeset by Computertype Limited
Printed by Colour Books Limited

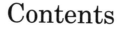

Contents

1 The Blow-In

One lovely winter evening, I'm curled up in my basket before a roaring fire.

There's the mother of all storms outside. Rain. Wind. Sleet. Snow on the way.

I turn over and curl up again. Fish-pie later. I love winter.

An hour later I wake up

Something is making a noise outside. Like 'Meow, Meow.'

I'm nodding off again when Missus Cook says to Mister Cook (I live with them), 'Did you hear a noise outside?'

He shakes his head but opens

MEOW MEOW

the door anyway. In blows a
plastic carry bag.

'It's a plastic bag!' he says.

He can be real smart – when
he tries hard.

There's that noise again. It's
coming from the bag.

'Let's see what it is,' he says.

I don't like this at all.

It could be anything. A snake? A cat-eating monster?

Has he never heard of snakes or cat-eating monsters?

I make sure I can make a quick exit. Just in case!

Missus Cook says, 'Look!'

I go a little nearer.

The pair of them are standing there with great big smiles.

What *have* they found?

'It's a kitten. A little kitten for you to play with.'

A kitten! A KITTEN!

That's all I need at my age. A silly little kitten. They'll expect **me** to look after it.

Well, no way.

The Cooks are *still* drooling. 'Isn't he beautiful?'

Actually it's a she, not a he.

And beautiful? Black and white and bits of orange all over the place.

Looks like the da was black and white and the ma was orange and this thing has turned out to be a real mess.

'He's purring!' says Mister.

Talk about being thick! Does he not know that all cats purr?

'He must be hungry,' says Missus Cook. 'I'll give him milk in Cookie's bowl.'

My bowl! Why **my** bowl? That's **mine**. It belongs to me.

Still, maybe if she gets some milk she'll go on her way.

I'll go back to sleep. When I wake up, she'll be gone.

I wake up after a lovely dream. At least I think it was lovely! I can't remember.

'Come and meet Curley,' says Missus Cook. 'That's what we're going to call her – look, she has a lovely little curl in the centre of her forehead. I know you'll both be great friends.'

She's STILL here!

I swish my tail. No reaction!

'Now we must go out to buy food. Curley has eaten all the supper and drunk all the milk.'

Nothing left? I'm starving to death. And dying of thirst.

The Cooks go out but they're soon blown back by the wind. Their umbrella is in bits.

'We can't go out tonight,' says Mister. 'That's some gale.'

The fire is going down and I
suppose there's no more fuel.

Any more bad news?

Yes! I'm shunted out of my
basket.

'I'm sure you won't mind,
Cookie,' says Missus Cook.
'But poor little Curley needs a
good warm place to sleep.

I swish my tail again!

Cold, hungry and thirsty,
I stretch out on a hard mat for
a sleepless night.

Through all this something
nags at my brain. I can't think
what. Well, this is no time for
walks down memory lane.

I'll get rid of her tomorrow.

2 Day One

I wake up dead tired.

The kitten! Is she still here?

She's not in her basket. Or on the sofa. Oh, no! She's on the dresser. With all the best plates.

A plate flies past. I catch it just in time.

'Be careful!' I cry. Another plate follows. I catch it too.

She knocks off a third one while I'm catching the second.

Smash! Crash! It's in bits on the floor.

That gives her a fright!

She leaps down and into her box, just as the Cooks come in.

'Coo-ee, Cookie, Curley…
What's going on? *My plates!*'

And me with a broken piece in my hand!

Don't look at me. Honest, I didn't break it. It's that kitten. Full of trouble she is.

No one listens. Too busy feeding Curley in **my** bowl. I get an old saucer Pity she didn't break that.

COOKIE

Now what's she's up to.

She's tearing threads out of the rug. The one the mouse used to chew up.

At least they can't blame me!

'Poor kitty,' says Missus Cook. 'She wants to play.'

'Cookie used to play with corks when he was young,' says Mister Cook. 'I think I know where they are.'

'What a long time ago that was,' Missus says. 'Poor Cookie. He's slowed down.'

Now they're all playing together! Grown-ups! Really!

Some memory still nags my brain. What can it be?

3 Up the Garden Path

Next day the Cooks go out.

'Mind Curley,' says Mister to me. 'If she gets out, she may not find her way back.'

Great! Super! I have an idea.

I'll take her into the garden next door. She's bound to get lost in the long grass.

'Tell you what,' I say to her. 'Let's go into the next door garden. Lovely flowers there.'

Flowers? In winter?

She's really a bit thick.

We go through the cat-flap and the hole in the hedge into

 Missus Drip's garden.

When she's looking for the flowers, I sneak away. I block up the hedge hole and go home.

The Cooks aren't back yet.

I drag my basket over to the cat-flap and hop into it. If she *does* get back, it won't be easy to push it aside with me in it!

Don't get me wrong. I've nothing against her. But she just doesn't fit in here.

Now I think I'll have a little
nap. In my own basket!

I am woken up by the Cooks.

'Where's Curley?' they say.
They rush around everywhere,
calling and carrying.

'*I'm* here.' I say.

All they say is, 'Why is your
basket before the cat-flap?'

I'm dumped out and it's put
back before the fire.

'She must have squeezed
out through this window.'

'Poor little thing. She's lost
again. Oh, why did we go out!'

Sob, sob. Doom and gloom.

All over a silly little kitten.

What's the world coming to?

29

Knock! Knock!

It's the awful Missus Drip
from next door. With Curley.

'I found her in the garden.
She must be a stray. Now I'm
very fond of cats ... *most* cats ...'

She glares and I slink behind
a chair. No love lost there. If
she comes near me, I'll sink my
teeth into her ankle.

'... but I can't keep her. My Arabella is a pedigree cat. She doesn't like common cats.'

What a lie! Arabella and I get on very well together.

'I thought you might like her. *Your* cat won't mind.'

Plan One bites the dust.

4 River Dance

Next day I ask Curley if she'd
like to come for a walk.

'Can't we stay by the fire?'

'On this lovely day!'

I look for – and find – an old
cardboard box.

'What's that for?'

'For a sail on the river.'

'In the box? Is it safe?'

'It's as calm as a mill-pond.'

At the river, I put her into the box and give it a small push.

Off it sails, down river. I see her anxious little face peering over the edge as she disappears.

I panic. *What have I done?*

Then I relax. The river *is* calm. The box will drift in to the bank. She'll get out and go back to her home. Cats always find their way home.

I hear a sudden shout.

'Hey, you, young shaver!'

I look around. A nasty old bulldog is waving an umbrella.

Young shaver? Me? Must be. There's no one else around.

'Where's that kitten?'

'I don't know,' I lie.

'I saw you. You put that poor
little kitten into a box and then
pushed it down the river.'

'I was taking her for a sail
but the box went off by itself.'

'A likely story!' He prods me,
sharply, with his umbrella.

'Come on, come on…no time
to lose…we have to save her.'

Dragging me, he shoots off.

What a run! I stub my toe on a rock, fall into a pool of water and am torn by a thorn bush.

We catch up with the box which has got stuck on a rock.

'Take my umbrella,' he says. 'Use it to drag in the box.'

'I have to go into the river?'

'Of course.'

36

'But I can't swim.'

'That's your bad luck.'

He looks as if he is about to hit me so I wade into the river.

Cold? It is icy!

I slip and I stumble as I get deeper and deeper. By the time I reach the box, I'm up to my waist in ice-cold water.

I hook the umbrella on to it
and drag it back to the bank.

The old codger takes his
umbrella and shakes it at me.

'Don't try that again or...'

I lope off before he finishes.

Curley trots after me. 'Where were you?' she asks.

'The box went off too fast.'

'I was scared. But I knew you'd come and rescue me.'

She almost said, 'My hero!'

I'm still stuck with her. Another fine mess!

5 Climbing High

I have to think of a new plan.

Meanwhile, I make myself scarce. Even the Cooks begin to notice. 'We never see anything of Cookie these days. I wonder if he's jealous?'

Me jealous? That's a cat laugh! I only want a *little* attention.

Today I don't make a quick get-away after dinner.

Curley tags along after me. She natters on about the clouds and the trees and the bushes...

She's a nice little thing – in the right place. Not *our* place!

All of a sudden, two huge
dogs appear from nowhere.
'Run!' I yell to her.

When I'm safe on top of a
wall, I look for her. Nowhere!
Then I hear a faint 'Meow'.

She's at the top of the tallest
tree for miles around. The dogs
are under it, barking like mad.

What am I to do?

I can't fight the dogs!

I'll go home. They'll get
tired and go off. She'll climb
down (she got up so she can get
down) and go to her old home.

The whole thing has *nothing* to do with me. *I* didn't ask her to come for a walk. *I* didn't lay on the dogs. *I* didn't tell her to climb up such a tall tree.

* * * *

A storm is blowing up. The Cooks sit by the fire and worry.

'It's not like Curley to be out this late,' says Missus Cook for the tenth time.

'No indeed,' says Mister.

If this goes on, I'll go mad!

'Remember the night she came to us,' says Missus Cook. 'It reminded me of the night we found Cookie. Remember, we opened the door and there he was – thin and wet and hungry.'

'Yes...and we took him in.
He ate everything in sight and
slept for days!'

That was what had nagged
me! My coming to the Cooks!

It had been deep in my
memory all this time. Now it
flooded back. They had taken
me in. Just as they did Curley.
And I had tried to push her out.

Suppose there had been a selfish cat here when I was let in. A cat who tried to get rid of me? What a terrible thought!

Five o'clock strikes. It's getting dark.

Mister Cook goes out into the garden. 'No sign.'

Missus wipes away a tear. 'At least we have Cookie…and it's his birthday tomorrow. I've baked him a cake.'

I cover my ears. This is getting worse and worse. I can bear it no longer. I dash over to the door and yell, 'Meow, meow.'

'Why doesn't he use the cat-flap?' says Mister, not moving.

I scratch at the door like mad until they finally get the message and open it. I go down the path, then back again to the kitchen. Several times.

'I think he wants us to follow him,' says Mister.

They get their coats and follow me. I lead them to the big tree. She's still up there, calling 'Meow, Meow.'

'It's Curley!' say the Cooks. 'You're safe! Come on down.'

But no way will she budge!

'Now what?' says Missus.

There's only thing for it. I'll have to climb up and get her.

It's not that I like climbing trees at my age (I don't like heights anyway). But a cat's got to do what a cat's got to do.

'Cookie, Cookie, mind yourself, it's a very tall tree,' shouts Mister as I shin up,
I try not to think about it.
Up. Up. Up.
The branches are thinning out as I climb. Mustn't fall and have to start again. Once is enough for this kind of caper.

Oops! I fall four meters as
my mind wanders. One of my
nine lives flashes before me. I
grab a branch. *Concentrate!*

Ah, there's Curley. Out at
the end of a branch.

Sticky bit here. No footholds.

Another branch to go. Almost make it. Then I slip. *Blast those footholds!*

I plunge down. Five meters. Another life gone forever.

I latch on to a stray branch.

I reclimb the five meters, and shout, 'Curley, I'm coming.'

Oh, oh! The branch is bending as I crawl out to her. I'll have to chance it. It might just take my weight and hers.

I reach out and grab her.

'Got you! Get on my back!'

'But I'll fall,' she wails.

'You big eejet,' I snarl at her. She must be more afraid of me than of falling. 'Get on my back or I'll drop you.'

That does it. As she gets on

my back, I say, 'Put your arms around my neck. Hold on tight.'

'We'll fall,' she sobs.

'We won't,' I say. 'But stop shaking or we'll both fall.'

As we start on the down trek,
I nearly make a fatal mistake.
I look down!
The ground is a mile away.
I see the tiny Cooks and a
crowd of ants milling around.
All looking up at me.

I nearly fall but manage to grab a branch. Another life goes by – have I any left?

Curley gives a little yelp.

Never look down, I repeat.

I start down. Backwards.

A voice floats up. 'Take it easy, Cookie. We don't want to lose you.'

I don't want to lose myself!

I continue down. Seventy meters...sixty...fifty...forty...thirty...twenty...

Careful now, I tell myself.

...ten meters. ZERO!

We're down! Ground underfoot. I'll never leave it again.

The Cooks rush forward.

'Well done,' says Missus.

'Old chap,' adds Mister.

Then it's TV, radio, press....

6 Home for Tea

Home at last. Super hot supper.
Birthday cake. Bowl of milk.
Basket before the fire.

   'Cookie, what *would* we do

without you?' say the Cooks.

My cup overflows.

Later, Curley gives me a great big smile. 'My hero! I knew you'd come.'

I've got quite fond of her. She trusts me. And she likes me.

'Welcome home,' I say. 'But we must settle one thing first.'

'What's that?'

'The pecking order.'

She stares. 'The what?'

'I'm Number One. You're Number Two. Never forget!

'And always remember I need my space. No crowding!'

* * * *

I think things are going to be okay from now on.

CHIMP CHAT

Now I'm going to tell you a little about the ape clan – there are four of us.

Gorillas are the largest. When they stand up, they're not quite as tall as a man but they're more powerful. But in spite of their great strength, they're gentle and won't attack you – if you leave them alone. They live in the forests of west Africa, along the Equator, where they get plenty of bananas to eat.

 What's wrong with the two odd-looking chimps on page 2?
*I gave you a clue last time I talked to you … chimps are **apes** – no tails!*

Frank Mulligan lives in Arklow with his wife Teresa and their five children.

This is his second book. The first was *Cookie the Cat*.

He is now working on 'Cookie' three.

Terry Myler is one of Ireland's best-known children's book illustrators. In addition to illustrating other writers' books, she has written two: *Drawing Made Easy* and *Drawing Made Very Easy*.